A MILLION *DIFFERENT* YOUs

A Short Story About Becoming Whole

Beyr Reyes

A MILLION DIFFERENT YOUs:
A Short Story About Becoming Whole
Beyr Reyes

Visit our Web site at
www.ShadeTreePublishing.com.

Contents

So then, each of us will give an account of ourselves to God.

Romans 14:12

A Day in the
Life of Rachael

Today started like any other day. Despite the puking dog with a fixation for crayons and the nasty toilet water that embraced my cell phone amidst my vigorous plunging, somehow, I managed—once again—to get everyone clothed, fed, and out the door on time before dumping myself into the driver's seat of big Bertha, our worn-out minivan.

While resting my head on the steering wheel, I contemplated my dangling red curls, trying to decide my next move. I *could* sneak back inside and hide my head in the pillows. Oh, how glorious that would be, given all my fatigue from a night of more tears than sleep. I picked up my head just enough to peer over the dash and glance around for any witnesses to my potential retreat.

Well crap. There *she* was; my perky neighbor sprawled out in her front yard, dressed in tight running clothes, and working hard (quite provocatively I might add) to stretch her legs before the morning's run. "How annoying."

No sooner had I rolled my eyes and muttered that thought, did the guilt slam me. In a feeble attempt to defuse the onslaught of remorse, I made a mental note to add "exercise more" to my to-do list; however, this superficial intention did nothing for the real conviction that was growing in the pit of my gut. I knew what was really going on here. God had been dealing with me over this particular lady, and more than once, I was supposed to invite her to church. Today, like all other days, I let my personal distaste for her get in the way. "Tomorrow, Lord... and this time, I promise." I resolved to pray for the woman until then as I put Bertha in reverse and backed onto the street. Praying was the least I could do, right?

OKAY... Coffee... That's what I need.

I decided that my usual pick-me-up would put things in proper motion and perspective. I took a right on Elm toward my favorite shop. While en route, I tried to put the haunting pang in my heart to rest and prove to God that my intentions back at the house were righteous. I recited a small prayer for my neighbor as promised, but it didn't take long for my own needs to eclipse any pleas for her, and I veered off into self-invocations. The weight of my world was almost too heavy to bear, and I desperately needed help. Here I was, Rachael, the one who helps everyone else, needing help myself.

The car must have been driving itself, because I was somewhere lost in prayer. My shallow preamble for the neighbor lady transitioned to deep intercession for myself.

A shrill honk jolted me back into the real world in just enough time to stop at the red light. I studied the rearview mirror searching for lingering evidence of my emotional distress. As if the dark circles were not bad enough, I saw that only one eye donned mascara. *Really?? Again??* Somewhat experienced at this now, I fished around in my purse for my emergency make-up stash with one hand while steering with the other. The other eye would surely get its turn at one of the next red lights.

Ten minutes later and after few final takes in the mirror, I yanked the keys from the ignition and made my way across the parking lot of the coffee house. Head down and trying to get one foot in front of the other, I scarcely noticed someone rescuing me from a faceplant with the front door. However, the bustling energy and rich aroma in the shop caused me to lift my head just in time to thank my pastor for his chivalry.

I opted to stand in line instead of finding a seat, for fear I'd get trapped in another commitment at church that, quote: "could benefit from your expertise,

Rachael." While I loved the idea of helping and serving others, I honestly didn't know where I would find the time or energy to do one more thing.

My take-out plan failed, as pastor scooted up behind me in line and wasted no time with his next favor. I couldn't find the courage to straight up say no, so I used my fallback plan and said the next best thing: "I'll pray about it, Pastor Jim." A brush of divine intervention must have painted me an escape, because just then, the cashier handed me my order. I darted out the door with both my coffee and those parting words.

The stiff, steamy brew certainly did the trick like always. I tackled my daunting to-do list, and the rest of the day passed without fail. Well, sort of anyway. There *was* that embarrassing grocery store incident when I dropped a family-size can of corn on my foot. I hoped that old Mrs. Hinkle, who was shopping in the same aisle, didn't hear me utter that shovelful of profanities afterward, but her raised eyebrow said otherwise. I sprinted toward the checkout, sure that I would catch some heat about it the next time I volunteered at the nursing home where she worked.

While driving home, happy to have all the day's tasks finally behind me and fueled with thankfulness now instead of caffeine, I wanted to check in with my husband. I reached for my phone, missed, and knocked it into the passenger side floor of the minivan. Certain that I could reach it, I extended my body while still trying to keep my eyes above the dash. Needing only one more inch, I lunged quickly, removing my eyes from the road for only a split second. But that was all it took. In that fraction of time, my lurch and consequential pull on the steering wheel caused the car to swerve off the road and plunge over a steep embankment.

What started out like most days, ended like no other.

More Than Millions

While absorbed in a dead-like sleep, I began to perceive an uncanny noise, like the blast of some sort of alarm. An automatic response to that sort of sound had me swinging my arms trying to reach the alarm clock. However, the only thing my hands found was the boundaries of a confined space. I was somewhere trapped and unable to move.

The shrillness of the siren grew and birthed a stirring in me. My thoughts became clearer, and I quickly realized I wasn't dreaming. The last thing I remembered was driving. *Is it a car horn? An emergency siren?* My thoughts ignited a panic. *Am I trapped? Paralyzed? Where exactly am I, anyway?*

I became increasingly rattled as the grave alarm continued to ring. Between the blasts, though, it was dead quiet. Eerily so. I wondered why it was taking so long to free me. Before I could attempt a scream, I heard someone else shout. "Wake up all you sleepers, and rise from the dead!" The voice was not familiar and lacked any hint of emotion. And here, I thought I'd already determined that I wasn't sleeping.

I felt the mighty words surge through me and create a deep vibration from within my bones, like they had become some sort of tuning fork humming a new song. Before I could respond, my body started a submissive ascent. Not sure who was doing the lifting, and still unable to see anything, or even my rescuer, I wondered if I were blind.

As I glided up, my vision proportionally improved. Everything went from black to light as my body emerged from the ground. *Was I in a hole or something?* It didn't make sense at first, but then it hit me when I caught a glimpse of my own tombstone passing by.

Oh My God—I'm DEAD!!! No...wait! How could I be dead? Wait... What???

(One might think that with all the church talk I'd heard over the years, that I would have recognized resurrection, but all I can say is nothing can prepare someone for this.)

Now reaching a considerable height in the air, I glanced around and saw other folks around me, making their glorious climb as well. Hundreds of souls looking like wisps of steam rising from a fresh loaf of bread. And then, in what seemed like a wink of an eye, I found myself standing among an unfathomable throng of people. Multitudes who were sleeping in the dust of the earth were now awake and gathered in some sort of ethereal place. A place indescribable, and yet very familiar.

Some people appeared confident while others confused, but *all* were herded around in an organized manner, separated almost supernaturally into flocks. It reminded me of ice cracking and how random lines would race across the surface, parting each icy fragment in an instant. Only this time, the lines were straight and driven by divine order. I surrendered myself to the flow of the traffic.

At the center of this place shone a brilliant light unlike any my eyes had ever seen. It was like looking directly at a white-hot sun without having to squint and still being able to see in exquisite detail. The last time I looked at something so bright, I needed eclipse glasses.

In the heart of the light sat the Lord God upon a great white throne surrounded by a couple dozen smaller thrones. Upon each of these smaller thrones sat the elders dressed in white with crowns of gold on their heads. Also around the throne were four creatures, and every time they gave glory, honor, or thanks to the Lord, the elders fell prostrate in worship. Dispersed throughout this place were thousands upon thousands of angelic beings ready to serve.

The beauty of the scene, as breathtaking as is was, paled in comparison to the splendor of the Lord God, though. Clothing white as snow and hair like pure wool, He sparkled more brilliantly than any gem or jewel. He was the purest of white light, without blemish or shadow, and yet His form was wholly discernable (an artistic impossibility outside the realm of this place). Inexplicable splendor. Every moment I beheld Him, my soul felt its worth, and I could have spent an eternity just gazing upon Him. An abrupt call to order interrupted my fixation on His exquisiteness.

"The time has come for the judging the dead," said the Lord, and immediately the heavenly assembly took on the look of a court room. All mankind, great and small, stood waiting before His throne.

After a prolonged, solemn silence, an elder announced, "Behold the Book of Life!" as an angel entered while carrying a large glowing object. The item looked like a combination between an ancient scroll I once saw in a museum and my granny's giant coffee-table Bible. I couldn't help but imagine this glowing book containing news clippings of weddings and births, just like hers. When the volume was finally opened, a reverent silence once again swept over the masses.

Another elder motioned, and a great fiery gulf was revealed in the distance. He declared, "Anyone whose name is not found written in the book will be thrown into the lake of fire." When finished with his proclamation, he bowed in worship along with the others.

Until now, the loveliness of this place had eclipsed the purpose for this solemn congregation. The ominous pit was a solid reminder. A reverent fear gripped me as I realized the gravity of the situation. There was no escaping what was coming next.

An angel then called my name and commanded me to approach the great throne. But I froze. I just stood there. Dumbfounded. *Surely there was someone else who could go first.*

Despite not wanting to step out (especially alone in front of all these people), I finally shoved my reluctance aside and eased forward out of the crowd. For some strange reason, though, a multitude of others stepped forth with me. I looked around and saw that I was accompanied by an untold number of identical-looking redheads.

Attempting to make some sense of what was going on, I dropped my head and stared in dismay at my feet. That's when a strange feeling came over me, like my spirit was swelling up out of my surroundings. For a split second, I could see this giant herd of redheads from above. I couldn't believe it! How could it be? There were millions upon millions of me standing around, and each one mirroring my own confusion.

The Sheep and the Goats

Unable to comprehend the entirety of the situation, I stood there, elbow-to-elbow with all of my doppelgangers. I wondered if they were wondering what I was wondering, and somewhere in all that circle logic, I my mind went down a rabbit hole.

The sound of the Lord asking one of the angels a question snapped me back to attention. His powerful voice washed over the crowd like a tidal wave. The inquiry was cryptic, but I could discern that it had something to do with a date and the issue of redemption.

Before the angel could answer, another beautiful being standing beside the throne stepped forward and reported the specific date. The angel smiled and nodded in affirmation.

I immediately recognized the date *and* the speaker. If anyone would know the date I was saved, it would have to be Jesus. And now, there He stood, gazing upon me with a soul-crushing love that whisked me away to the memory of when I first found Him. Our eyes were locked like doves as we reminisced that tender moment together.

The commotion of millions of people stirring about caused me to lose concentration and focus instead on not stumbling amidst all the movement. Angels were directing the herd of Rachaels to position themselves before the throne, those versions prior to the recorded date toward its left, and those after toward its right. The Lord then commanded the collection to separate completely into two groups. When He did this, the sea of redheads split, reminding me of Moses parting the Red Sea.

The group on the left of the throne was massive and too numerous to count. Most had unhappy and stressed looks on their faces. On the contrary, the group on the right was much smaller, perhaps a tenth of all the versions total, and their faces had a slight glow (some more than others). All of their faces changed, though, after what they heard next.

"As it was written, He will put the sheep on His right and the goats on His left," an elder declared.

And the Lord continued: "I will judge between one animal of the flock and another, separating the sheep from the goats. Behold! I will judge the living from the dead."

Dead and Gone

The two groups clung to the uncomfortable moment of silence as if trying to postpone the drop of an axe.

Without turning toward them or even gazing in their direction, the Lord first addressed the massive group on His left.

"Did I not say that the wicked will not stand in the judgment, nor sinners in the assembly of the righteous?

"When mankind was born, they inherited the stain of original sin, then as they lived, their sin multiplied. Because the wage of sin is death, a life must be given for sin's payment. It is not My desire should anyone perish, so I created a means of salvation for all mankind—my Son, Jesus the Christ."

At the very mention of *His* name, the angels cried out in unison, "Holy, Holy, Holy is the Lamb of God who takes away the sin of the world." All the elders followed suit and bowed in worship.

"I sent my Son as your replacement in death. All you had to do was accept the offer. To be born again, not of flesh, but of My spirit, who gives life and sets you free from this law of sin and death. Had you believed and accepted Christ as your Savior like the group you see across from you," and the Lord motioned to the group on His right, "you would have been sealed for eternal life with Me. But alas, you did not. And now, YOUR own death will be the payment for YOUR sin."

I was still trying to reconcile the pronouncement of death over the other versions of myself when the Lord turned slowly and looked directly at me.

"This is the judgement of the dead. I declare that flesh and blood cannot inherit the kingdom of God, nor does the perishable inherit the imperishable."

After the Lord said this, I looked across the divide at the crowd of my selves disappearing. Those sinful Rachaels whose name was not found written in the Book of Life were being cast into the lake of fire. Feelings of both grief and relief played tug-o-war with my heart.

Once the purge was finished, an elder rose from his throne and declared, "The tares are gathered and burned in the fire, and now, as it was written, the Lord will judge between the fat and lean sheep," then he bowed to the ground shouting, "Amen! Hallelujah!"

The Lord's penetrating eyes were locked onto mine. "My child, the former things are gone. Now behold your final judgement."

The First Thing, First

Now, really confused and a little fearful for what would happen next, especially considering that multitudes of my selves just disappeared, I started to wonder if I were next. *What did the Lord mean by 'final judgement?'* I knew I was saved, but the looming unknown worried me. And not to mention, I still couldn't get a handle on the purpose of all these versions of myself.

The Lord surveyed the remaining group of us Rachaels. I felt like one little ewe among a horde of identical ones standing before my Shepard. I looked over the flock and chuckled at my revelation… "a million different *yous*…"

"The time has come for the rewarding of His servant," announced an elder while all the others bowed in worship and shouted their praises.

"I, the Lord, search the heart and test the mind, to give every man according to his ways, the fruit of his deeds."

Then the Lord ordered each version of me to give an account for herself, starting with Rachael #1.

Unsure if He meant me or one of the other Rachaels, I just stood there waiting to see. I was relieved when one of the other Rachaels stepped forward, and I could now see that she had something written on her forehead. As a matter of fact, every version of myself had some sort of label, and Rachael #1's was "Rachael the Reborn."

"I am Rachael the Reborn. I am the Rachael at the altar giving my heart to Christ. The Lord made me a new creation and placed His spirit on me."

All the emotion I experienced in that little country church flooded me as I relived the account. All that forgiveness and love… somehow over the years, I had managed to forget the depths of it. *How does that even happen?* I didn't have much time to contemplate an answer because the Lord began to speak.

Looking again at me, He said, "You were reborn into a new life and received My spirit to help you along the way. Let us hear what you did with your new life and all the gifts I gave you. Each of you will give an account of yourself to me. To whom much was given, much will be required."

Judgement by All Accounts

This was my final hearing. A time to review my past and plead my case, that I may be tried and found faithful.

Every person, whether it be friend, family, or stranger, who had ever formed an opinion of my character or my deeds, thereby formulated a different version of me, and one by one these other Rachaels (my great cloud of witnesses) began testifying. As if reading my confusion, the Lord took a timeout to explain: "All of this according My Word, which declared that your honesty will testify for you in your future; your own mouth to condemn you, and your own lips to testify against you. For with the judgment you pronounce, you will be judged, and with the measure you use, you will be measured."

Oh my... My heart sank.

I could see this wouldn't be your regular courtroom trial here... I would be the prosecutor, defendant, and evidence all wrapped up into one.

Each Rachael proceeded to give her testimony, one by one. I watched my life play out before me as each version of myself gave a different account of it. I had heard of people who supposedly died and came back with stories about seeing their life flash before their eyes, but this was something on a whole different level. (And unlike them, I totally missed any opportunity to sell millions of books about *my* experience...)

Each report varied in tone and theme, and came in no particular order. Several of the versions, like "Rachael the Distracted" (who was known by the man I unknowingly cut off while driving and applying mascara at the same time) had a lot of me-too's step up and give similar reports.

Some of the accounts testified about my faithfulness and good works. For example, "Rachael the Faithful" (known by my pastor) was the faithful attendee, faithful tither, and faithful volunteer. "Rachael the Doer" was known by Mrs. Hinkle from the nursing home I volunteered at each week. This lady had also seen me serving at the soup kitchen, dispensing coats to the shivering homeless, and hammering nails with the local home-building organization; and in case I had any doubts—yes, she had indeed heard me cussing in the grocery store and this Rachael proceeded to tell everyone about my potty mouth.

The most flattering account came from Rachael known by the many strangers I prayed with after getting saved: the man on the bus no one else would even look at, the lady crying in the oncology waiting room, the cashier at the thrift store, and so on. The fire of God filled this Rachael's bones, and she couldn't stop telling people how awesome her sweet Jesus is. Listening to her made me want to get saved all over again.

My weaknesses and offences were made ever-so apparent in several accounts. One of the Rachaels readily shared the gospel with strangers, but was too scared to share with friends or family, *and especially*, a certain neighbor. Another Rachael was known by my debauchery-ridden cousin. To him, I was the uptight church lady spewing all the religious rhetoric at the family events. Many times, desperate for answers and confirmation that God was real, he was secretly looking to me for hope and truth, but I was too busy trying to keep his immorality from soiling my reputation. This was the version of me who let my cousin die unsaved because of too little love for the lost and too much love for self-righteousness.

The biggest surprise during my hearing was all the false accusations. I was utterly shocked at how many people had straight-up lied about me or had misinterpreted situations and then led others to spend years thinking I had wronged or forsaken them. So many Rachaels who were unfairly hated and misunderstood! My justice-driven heart felt like it would explode, and all I could think about was finding those people and fixing everything. Like that would help, though, especially at this point...

The most embarrassing of all the accounts was the Rachael known only by my innermost self. This version of me was consumed with having my own way. She was motivated by lustful desires, power and notoriety, revenge-seeking, etc. This Rachael was my sinful flesh that I secretly fed instead of putting to death.

Some accounts took longer than others, but none ever got in a hurry to finish. In this place, time was not an issue; if it took a thousand years, then that would be okay. (After all, how do a thousand years measure against eternity?) And in this trial, there was certainly enough time for judgement by all accounts.

Blinded Eyes That Now See

Eventually, all the other versions of myself had given their account, and only I remained. The Lord permitted me some time to reflect upon the testimonies defining my life. I sensed He was patiently waiting for me to come fully to repentance and understanding. The time had come for me to acknowledge my good deeds *and* my iniquities.

I took a moment to let the experience soak in.

Whereas before, I had perceived my life to be one way, now I had a higher perspective. The words "double-minded" and "two-faced" had all new meanings.

For the first time ever, I saw my *real* self, as everything hidden in darkness had been brought to light. The motives of my heart were exposed, even the ones hidden behind my good deeds, and as my awareness grew, so did my regrets and shame. Now laid open for all to see were my lost opportunities, unknown betrayals, and sins of omission. Needless to say, I was crushed by all the occasions that I had failed to share the gospel. Many times, I had denied Christ, although not directly like Peter, but certainly in my intentions.

Some accounts burned extra deep, like "Rachael the Wife" and how I'd hurt my husband at times without knowing it. And how he knew about my inner burdens and spent hours hidden away in prayer for me, only to be falsely accused of other things.

Other accounts totally gutted me, like when I saw myself forsake the innocent love of my five-year-old son, and how I often exchanged opportunities to be with him for serving others. Sometimes he needed my help too, and other times, he just needed his Mommy to keep him company while he played. How often I had denied him one of the things he loved most in his little world—*my attention.*

As much as my born-again selves were hard to stomach, I shuddered at the thoughts of watching all the other accounts from my pre-Jesus years. *Can't even imagine that agony.* Definitely thankful for *that* mercy.

Yes, when I was born again, I was made a new, but I wished I would've worked harder to lay aside my old ways, to have been an example of Jesus to the world instead of allowing the world to shape me. I could've been a brighter light to all those who were lost in the grips of darkness and death.

Don't get me wrong—I did a lot of good, but oh, how much more I could have done for the Lord! And why in the world was I sometimes nicer and more patient with strangers than with my own family?

Hind-sight was 20/20, and now my blinded eyes could spiritually see. My life was a stained-glass window held together by a blood-colored frame.

Becoming One With God

Clearly, I was a Rachael with one faith, yet wholly divided. *How did I become so fractured?* I felt as though I would fall to pieces there before the throne.

"Even so, the body is not made up of one part, but of many, and each member belongs to all the others," said the Lord, His tone gentle yet unyielding.

He continued: "My purpose has always been to bring unity to the body, thus making peace and reconciling the whole back to Myself.

"I will put your selves into My fire; I will refine them like silver and test them like gold. The fire will test the quality of each one's work. For all that survives, you will be rewarded; but, for what is burned up, you will suffer loss, yet will still be saved—even though only as one escaping through the flames. Through the process, you will be transfigured and transformed, granted the whole measure of My fullness, and then united with Me in spirit."

The Lord then commanded me to stand. Only now did I realize that I had been on my knees ever since the testimonies had begun.

A vast incomprehensible light from the throne reached out and consumed all the versions of me. Each one burned with a different brilliance of light according to its measure of Christ.

In the end, only a single Rachael remained. I had undergone my final convergence. My face shone like the sun, and my garments were as white as pure snow. I was beautiful beyond measure.

I stood before the throne, awaiting a response from the Lord. I watched His eyes adore me. Without hesitation, He rose from His great throne, rushed to me, and took my hands.

"I call you Temima, which means whole," He said, and then with a gentle brush of His finger, He wrote the new name on my forehead. "No longer a million different yous, you are now a single ewe returned to Me."

And all of heaven burst into rejoicing with Him.

***

Let us rejoice and be glad and give Him glory! For the wedding of the Lamb has come, and His bride has made herself ready. Revelation 19:7

Review Request

I hope you have enjoyed this short story about becoming whole. If so, then please let other readers know. Let's share the knowledge so people can pull themselves together and be transformed by the Word of God and the renewing of their mind.

About the Author

BEYR REYES received her doctorate degree in biomedical science. She has produced over 200 publications in science, medicine, and Christian genres. In addition, she has worked in the drug industry since 2005 as a regulatory writer for major international pharmaceutical and biotech companies. (Beyr Reyes is Jennifer Minigh's pen name for the Christian genre.)

You can contact Beyr Reyes via email, Twitter, or Facebook:

Beyr.Reyes@ShadeTreePublishing.com
@JenniferMinigh
Facebook.com/Jennifer.Minigh

489: A Short Story about Forgiveness

2016 CSPA Book of the Year
in General Fiction

Loaded with plot twists and surprises, this short story delivers a powerful message about forgiveness and how our lives affect other people, even those we don't know. Widely endorsed by therapists, this book helps readers to be set free from the bondage of unforgiveness.

Renewable Energy: A Short Story about Second Chances

The stories of the Bible from an alien perspective, *Renewable Energy* explores the purpose of life and how to get a second chance at it while being caught in the middle of a great battle for "soular" energy.

The Big Picture

2011 Readers' Favorite Bronze Award

Most folks know the stories about Creation, the Jewish nation, and Jesus, but they don't know how all these things are connected. *The Big Picture* provides a broad perspective of the Bible that will help the beginner place events and their purposes together. For the readers who always have their heads buried in certain passages, this book is a refreshing step back to help illuminate the big picture.

Subject Your Flesh

2014 CSPA e-Book of the Year

Need to get control of your life? Tired of constant dieting? Fed up with bad habits? Subjection is the answer that lasts. Learn how to eradicate the problem areas in your life. Take control of your flesh and turn your life around using the Word of God.

Fast Answers:
Fasting Plans for Specific Prayer Needs

Fast Answers has individualized fasting plans with a clear starting point, destination, and goal. The plans come in 1-, 3-, or 7-day varieties and are tailored for specific prayer needs. This book is designed to help people get answers and resolve problems by drawing closer to God through fasting.

Make a Choice

2011 Readers' Favorite Silver Award

What do you believe and how do you show it? *Make a Choice* is designed to challenge your foundational beliefs and then challenge you to stand on them. All along the way, you will make decisions that will affect your life forever.